For my children:
Anastasia, Olivia, and Henry Benedict,
with love

Published by Dial Books
A Division of Penguin Books USA Inc.
375 Hudson Street
New York, New York 10014
Conceived and produced by Breslich & Foss, London
Copyright © 1993 by Breslich & Foss
All rights reserved
Printed in Singapore
Designed by Roger Daniels
1 3 5 7 9 10 8 6 4 2

Library of Congress Cataloging in Publication Data
Bolton, Linda
Hidden pictures/Linda Bolton
p. cm.
Summary: Paintings and other works of art containing hidden pictures or
messages introduce a variety of artists, both famous and unidentified.
Includes projects for making hidden pictures.
ISBN 0–8037–1378–9
1. Puzzles in art—Juvenile literature. 2. Art—Themes, motives—Juvenile
literature. [1. Puzzles in art. 2. Picture puzzles. 3. Art appreciation.] I. Title.
N7560.B65 1993 701'.1—dc20 92–10528 CIP AC

LINDA BOLTON teaches architecture and art history, and
has written books on Gauguin, Degas, and Manet.
She studied art history at both the University of
East Anglia and Birkbeck College, London.

Linda Bolton

Hidden Pictures

Dial Books New York

INTRODUCTION

How does a picture of a monster turn into a prince's face right before your eyes? How can a waterfall also be the beard of a giant, or a swirl of lines and curves really be the faces of four famous people? Did you know that there are some pictures that can only be seen correctly through a tube of reflecting paper?

Every picture tells a story, but some pictures tell more than one—*if* you know exactly where and how to look. Many famous artists, as well as unfamiliar or anonymous ones, have incorporated secrets, messages, and clues into their pictures to confuse or enlighten viewers. Sometimes these messages or secrets have been warnings or reminders, other times they have documented an event, and on occasion they have just been for fun. Often artists have depicted scenes from the world around them to show how the same thing can look entirely different with very little change, depending on what our eyes and minds choose to see.

Hidden Pictures is a fascinating journey into the magical world of art. Readers will be introduced to a range of artists spanning several centuries, including Gauguin, Picasso, and Leonardo da Vinci, as well as examples of every type of visual riddle. These include anamorphic pictures, which are images that can only be viewed correctly from a certain angle; distorted pictures that need the assistance of the special mirror found at the back of the book; and pictures that make us question what the artist intended us to see. In addition to following the clues and solving the puzzles of other artists, readers can make their own secret, puzzling, and mysterious pictures by following special project instructions.

So turn the pages and see how many hidden pictures you can find and create!

WHEN IS A ROOM
NOT A ROOM?

When it is a face. The twentieth-century Spanish painter Salvador Dali created this unusual picture from two completely different images. The title of the picture is "The Face of Mae West." Do you see why?

Dali took a photograph of the famous Hollywood film star Mae West and painted a room over the top of it. Mae West's lips have become a sofa, and her nose has become a mantelpiece. Her eyes have become two pictures on the wall, and her chin is the four steps at the entrance of the room. The artist has created an illusion of depth that the room needs by painting the floorboards wide at the bottom of the picture and narrow toward the middle. So if you focus on the floorboards, you will see a room, and by focusing on the eyes, nose, and mouth, you will see a face.

WHAT IS THE
AMBASSADORS' SECRET?

This painting by Hans Holbein the Younger, called "The Ambassadors," looks very ordinary. . . . But look at the bottom of the picture. What is the object by the ambassadors' feet?

Below is a detail of the strange shape. If you turn the right-hand side of the book toward you, and put your nose against the side of the page, you will be able to see it. It may also help to close your right eye.

The distorted shape is actually a skull. It is an example of an anamorphic picture, since it must be viewed from a specific angle to be seen clearly. Artists often painted skulls and skeletons in their pictures if they were painting portraits of rich and powerful people, as a reminder that money and importance cannot save anyone from eventually dying.

(Hint: The straight bottom edge is the jawbone, and the curve on the upper right is the back of the head.)

PORTRAIT OF AN ARTIST

This painting by the nineteenth-century French artist Paul Gauguin is called "Old Women at Arles." The old women are walking through the garden, but someone else is there too. . . . Can you see where?

Gauguin deliberately painted a picture of himself in the bush at the forefront of the picture. If you look carefully, you can make out his eyes, nose, and mouth.

It is possible that Gauguin did this to show his role as the artist—observing but not being observed.

WHO IS IN THE PICTURE?

These two pictures by an unknown artist—one a portrait of Mary, Queen of Scots, and the other of a skull—are, in fact, the same painting, but it has been photographed from two different angles. If you saw the painting and looked at it from the right-hand side, you would be able to see this grinning death's head, instead of the Queen's face that you can see from the left-hand side.

Mary, Queen of Scots was hated by the English Queen, Elizabeth I (1558–1603), who suspected Mary of plotting to overthrow her and take her throne. When a plot was discovered by one of Elizabeth's ministers in 1586, she had Mary executed for treason. This may be why the artist has twinned her portrait with a skull.

To make your own double picture, turn to page 47.

THE ANIMAL MAN

This extraordinary painting, entitled "Earth," by the sixteenth-century Italian artist Giuseppe Arcimboldo, shows a group of animals stacked on top of each other. If you look closely, you can see a camel, a bear, a lion, a sheep, a monkey, a horse, and many others. But there is also another picture here.

The animals have been positioned in such a way that they form the profile of a man's head. Once you have managed to trace the man's profile, your brain will adjust to the fact that this picture can be seen in two ways, and your eyes will "switch" back and forth.

(The fox's open mouth is a man's eye, the hare on the fox's back is a man's nose, and the leopard's head is a man's chin. The man and the elephant share the same ear!)

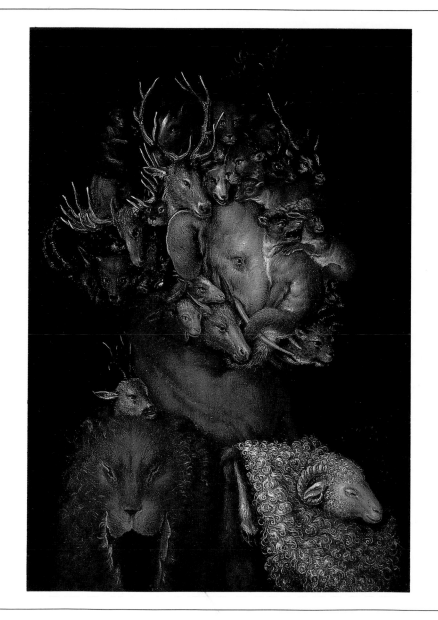

THE MUSICIANS'
BEST FRIEND

This painting, by twentieth-century Spanish artist Pablo Picasso, is called "Three Musicians." Although Picasso has not painted his musicians in a very lifelike way, we can certainly see that the figure on the left-hand side in the white pointed hat is playing a pipe, the central figure in the harlequin costume is playing the guitar, and the dark figure on the right has a music book. But there is something else in the picture. . . . Can you see what it is?

(Hint: Look for ears and a tail.)

HOW MANY PEOPLE IN THE PICTURE?

The picture on the opposite page, by the fifteenth-century Dutch artist Jan van Eyck, is called "The Arnolfini Marriage." How many people are there?

To find out, look below at a close-up of the curved mirror that appears on the wall behind the bride and groom. You will see that two additional people are reflected: One is the priest who is marrying the couple, and the other is the artist, who has signed "Johannes de eyck fuit hic" ("Jan van Eyck was present") above the mirror and written the date, 1434. This was probably used to record the marriage, just as a photo would today.

MIRROR IMAGE— OR IS IT?

This is a self-portrait by the sixteenth-century artist Parmigianino. There is something different about it. Can you see what it is?

To draw a self-portrait, any artist would need to look in a mirror, but here Parmigianino has chosen a convex mirror (a mirror that curves out, like the bottom of a spoon), and painted the distorted reflection he saw in it. Look at the size of the hand—it is much too large for the head and body. However, its large size may show the importance of the artist's hand: Without it, he could not draw or paint.

FRIEND OR FOE?

This painting by sixteenth-century artist William Scrots seems to be a frightening-looking person with a squashed face and long nose. It is hanging in the National Portrait Gallery in London, England, where if you look at the painting through a special peephole, the picture transforms itself. For the same effect, open the book up so that the picture is flat. Hold it upright, put your nose against the edge of the right-hand page, and close one eye. What do you see?

   This is a painting of King Edward VI, son of King Henry VIII of England. It was painted in

1546, the year before Edward became king. The artist painted him like this because he wanted to demonstrate his skill by painting something that could be seen in two ways. When this picture was first displayed, it was considered a marvel, and people flocked to the palace to see it. The Latin lettering and numerals that are painted around the prince's head indicate that he was nine years old at the time of the portrait.

PUZZLING PICTURES

It isn't possible for us to see the true shape of this distorted picture by using only our eyes. To see it, we need some help—from the reflective silver paper you will find at the back of this book. Detach the paper by tearing or cutting along the perforated edge, and roll it into a tube. The diameter of the tube should be about the same size as the circle in the middle of the opposite picture. (If you want, you can put a strip of tape down the long side of the tube to hold it together more easily.) Now stand the tube on top of the circle in the middle of the picture, and look into it. Don't look down it as if it were a telescope, but look at the outside. Can you figure out what this picture is? (See page 56 for the answer.)

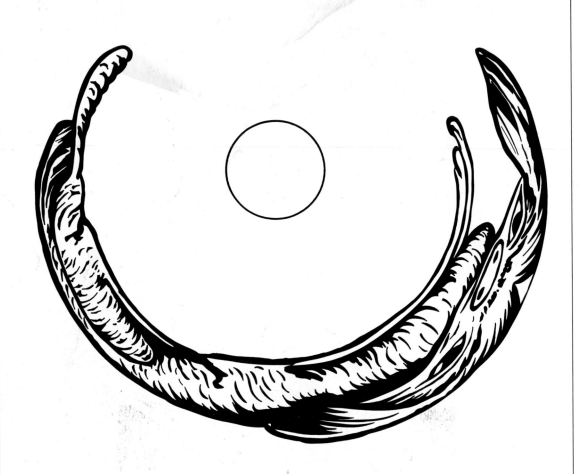

What is curled up at the bottom of the page? Place your rolled-up reflecting paper on the center circle to find out. (See page 56 for the answer.)

Can you figure out this strange design? Use your reflecting paper to find out what it is. (See page 56 for the answer.)

This beautiful, intricate pattern is hiding something. To transform it, place your rolled-up reflecting paper over the black circle in the center. (See page 56 for the answer.)

Use your rolled-up reflecting paper to make this swirl of colors fall into shape. Who is there? (See page 56 for the answer.)

Look into these swirling lines of color. Can you make out anything? Place your rolled-up reflecting paper over the orange circle in the center of the picture. What can you see now?

Unlike other pictures of this type, this one is a complete circle so you will have to turn the whole book around in order to see all of it. When you do this, you will find some clues to tell you who these two people could be. Can you see a crown and scepter? Can you see a chest of coins? Turn to page 56 to find out who these people are.

What can you see on the opposite page? There is clearly a skull close to the center of the picture, but what is above it? To find out, turn the book upside down and place the rolled-up reflecting paper on the circle containing the skull.

Now you can see that it is a portrait of a man—King Charles I of England, who was beheaded in 1649. This picture was painted in 1660, so the anonymous artist would have known of Charles's death, and painted the skull to remind people of his fate.

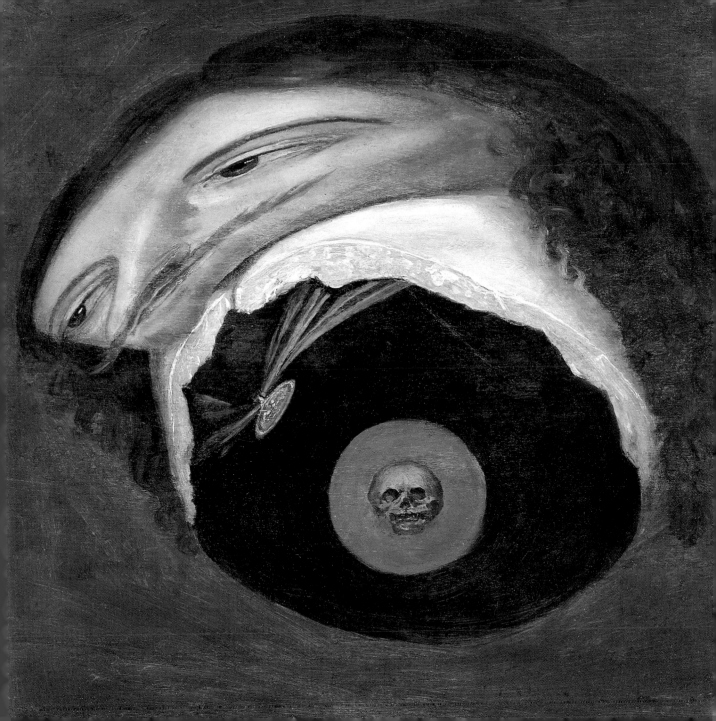

This puzzling picture was painted by an unknown nineteenth-century artist. What do you think it is? Use your rolled-up reflecting paper to find out. (See page 56 for the answer.)

FIND THE FACES

The woodcut that appears on the following pages was made in the sixteenth century by an artist named Erhard Schon. Seen from the front it looks like a landscape with small figures, ships, and buildings. But if you open the book all the way so that the picture is flat, hold it upright, and put your nose against the edge of the right-hand page, it will turn into something entirely different. Can you see what? (Closing one eye may help you to see it more clearly.)

There are actually three faces—two facing to the left and one facing to the right. They are the faces of three of the most powerful men in Europe during the sixteenth century: Ferdinand I, Pope Paul III, and Francis I. This is an example of an anamorphic—or distorted—picture.

STRANGE FACE

This picture entitled "Paranoiac Figure" by Salvador Dali seems to be of a group of people sitting on the ground outside a round hut, with some bushes in the background. But look again, carefully. . . . It is a picture of something else as well. What is it? Turn the book ninety degrees to the right to find out.

Now you can see that it is a picture of a human face. The bushes in the picture's background have turned into hair, the hut has become a cheek, and the large white jar furthest to the right has become the chin. The angle of the nose is made by the reclining figure and another, smaller white jar.

Dali had the idea for this picture when he saw a photograph of a group of people sitting beside a hut. He saw that, by chance, the people were positioned in such a way that they looked like the outline of a face, so he copied the photograph to make the painting.

37

FLYING FISH,
SWIMMING BIRDS

This painting, "Sky and Water I," is by the twentieth-century Dutch artist Maurits Cornelis Escher. Look at the center of the diamond shape. What do you see?

At the top of the picture you can clearly see a black bird flying in a white sky, and at the bottom you can see a white fish swimming in a black sea. But as your eye moves up and down the picture, the birds and fish seem to merge together. The artist has achieved this effect by gradually decreasing the details of the feathers and scales, and concentrating only on the shapes of the creatures, so that they fit together in the center of the painting like pieces of a jigsaw puzzle. The background sky and sea have disappeared—so the fish seem to be flying, and the birds to be swimming.

LANDSCAPE OR GIANT?

At first glance this picture by the seventeenth-century artist Josse de Momper looks like the face of a giant. But try covering the top half of the picture. What do you see? Now slowly move your hand away.

The beard of the giant is also a bridge with a waterfall flowing underneath. His nose is made by a tower, his eyes are two houses, his forehead a mountaintop, and his hair various trees. Which do you see when you look at the picture? . . . A face or a landscape? Or both?

SUNSET COMES DOWN

Look at the picture on the opposite page. It was painted by the twentieth-century Belgian artist René Magritte. He called the picture "Evening Falls." Why do you think he gave it this title?

Clearly, it is a picture of a broken window, and outside we can see the setting sun and a landscape with hills and trees. But take a look at the broken glass inside the room. . . . The same landscape and sun are on the pieces of broken glass. Do you think the sunset that we see out of the window is supposed to be a real one? . . . Or just another picture of one? It seems that the artist was having fun—playing with the viewer's idea of what is real and what is not.

43

LEONARDO DA VINCI'S
MIRROR WRITING

Can you read the writing above? It is deliberately written backward, and it can only be read with the help of a mirror. If you hold the writing up to face your reflecting paper, the words will be shown correctly.

The artist Leonardo da Vinci wrote these words over five hundred years ago—they are in Italian, so you may have trouble reading them. Leonardo da Vinci was a scientist, as well as a painter, and he kept secret notebooks in which he wrote down his theories and ideas in mirror writing. These notebooks contain drawings of his attempts to create the first flying machine and his plans for building the first telescope. One of his theories was that the earth goes around the sun. Today, everyone knows this is true, but in Leonardo's time it was thought that the sun went around the earth, and anyone who dared to suggest anything else would have been considered very wicked, imprisoned, and perhaps even put to death. So Leonardo was very careful to keep his ideas to himself.

MAKE YOUR OWN
MIRROR WRITING

Perhaps, like Leonardo, you have some secrets. . . . So why not try keeping your own notebook with mirror writing. It's difficult at first, but the more you practice, the easier it becomes. With the help of your reflecting paper, read the example below. Now try writing some of your own, forming the letters from right to left, and placing your words from right to left on each line. Check in your reflecting paper to see if you have all the letters the right—or wrong—way around.

HIDDEN PICTURES ARE FUN!

MAKE YOUR OWN DOUBLE PICTURE

1 Put a piece of tracing paper over the pictures of the wild boar and the dragon on the following pages and trace over them using a pencil, including details such as their eyes, as well as the vertical lines.

2 Transfer your drawings to plain paper by turning the tracing paper facedown onto it and scribbling over the back of your tracings with a soft pencil. When you remove the tracing paper, you will be left with faint pictures of the dragon and boar, although they will now be facing in the opposite direction.

3 Go over the outlines with a felt-tipped pen, and color in your pictures, adding a background color if you want.

4 Take a piece of paper and draw a rectangle 12″ wide by 4″ high. Draw vertical lines an inch apart inside it to make 12 sections. Put a pencil cross in every other section.

5 Slice each of your pictures into 6 strips, along the vertical lines you have marked. Be sure to keep the strips in order so the pictures look as they did before you cut them.

6 Glue the 6 strips of the boar onto your marked rectangle, going from left to right, using every section marked with a cross.

7 Glue the strips of the dragon into the spaces remaining, also going from left to right.

8 Now cut your rectangle out, fold it in and out like a fan along the 12 original lines you had drawn, and stand it up on a flat surface. If you look at it from one side you will see the boar, and from the other you will see the dragon.

WILD BOAR

48

DRAGON

MAKE YOUR OWN
PUZZLING PICTURE

1 Look at the camel drawn in the square grid. The vertical lines on the grid are numbered 0 through 10, and the horizontal lines are marked A through K. These letters and numbers give us "grid" references, like a map—note the crosses where the shapes intersect with the grid lines.

2 Trace the circular grid carefully, and paste the traced grid onto a piece of construction paper or a poster board. Make sure that you have written in the letters A through K and the numbers 0 through 10 in the right places.

3 Now, using the numbered and lettered lines to help you, put the crosses on the square grid in corresponding places on your traced circular grid. Remember that the crosses will be much farther apart

on this grid than they were on the square grid.

4 Connect the crosses, using a soft pencil. Keep checking the camel in the square grid as you go—the one you are drawing is upside down as well as distorted, so do not be surprised if it looks odd. When you have connected all the lines between crosses, you can use the grid reference points to help you complete the details in the drawing such as the eyes and mouth.

5 Take your reflecting tube and look at your camel to check that your drawing is correct. (You can also look at the distorted camel shown on page 56.) If it is, and what you see in your tube is like the camel in the square grid, then use a felt-tipped pen to darken the outline, and then color it.

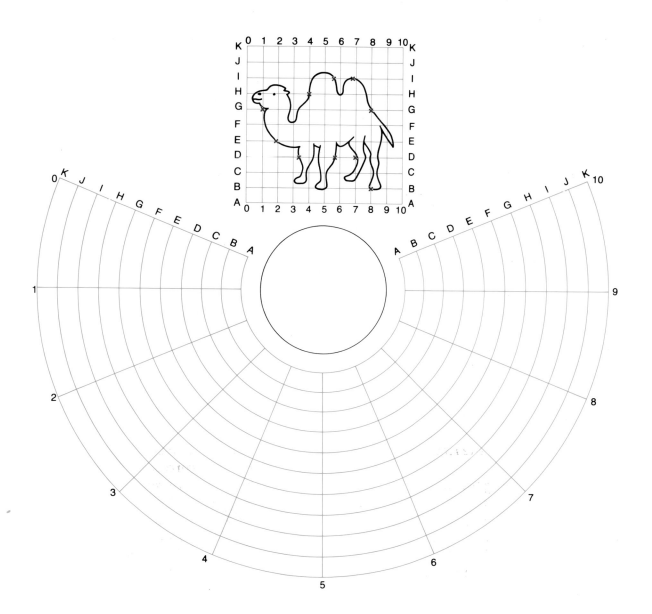

51

MAKE YOUR OWN
SECRET WRITING

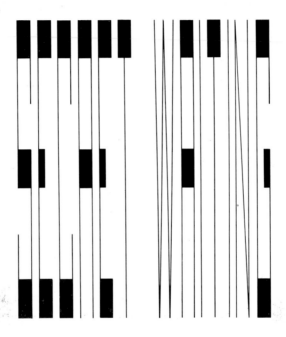

Can you read this? To make sense of it, place the bottom edge of the book underneath your chin, tilt the top of the book downward, and close one eye. You will then see these shapes in the correct perspective and be able to read the message.

Just as with the picture that appears on page 21 or the skull that appears on page 7, this writing is anamorphic—it must be seen from a certain angle in order to be read.

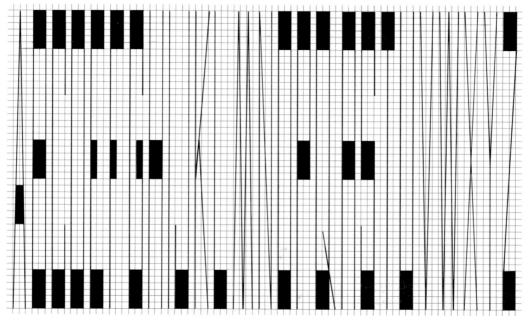

A B C D E F G H I J K L M N O P Q R S T U V W X Y Z

To make your own "secret writing," use the elongated alphabet above. Take some tracing paper, and trace off the letters of your name or of any words you choose. By using a piece of graph paper with larger squares but keeping the same proportions as the letters shown here, you can plot even larger and more distorted letters—this will keep your messages all the more hidden!

ALL DRESSED AND READY TO GO

The front cover of this book is yet another puzzling picture that can be seen with the reflecting paper. Turn the front cover upside down, and place your rolled-up reflecting paper on the red circle in the center of the pattern. What do you see?

This picture, entitled "Portrait of a Standing Man," is by the seventeenth-century Scandinavian artist Johann Konig. The elegantly dressed man is standing on a tiled floor in front of a colonnade.

CLEVER CREATURES

The artwork that appears at the front and back of this book is by the Dutch artist Maurits Cornelis Escher. Look at it closely. What do you see? Strange yellow creatures on a black background? Look again. Can you see black creatures, facing in the opposite direction?

There is, in fact, no real background to this picture at all. The creatures are mythical winged panthers, drawn so that they fit together like a jigsaw puzzle.

HIDDEN PICTURES ARE EVERYWHERE

It is not only artists who can see more than one thing when they look at a landscape or a face or a group of animals or a gathering of people. . . . Everyone at one time or another has had to look twice at something to decide what it really is. Different angles, different lighting, as well as memories of past images, all contribute to how we see something. The experience of looking at a cloud and seeing a face, for example, is common to us all.

By distorting a figure, altering perspective, or hiding something so that it is not immediately obvious, artists make us look—and think—again, and remind us that sometimes we must question what we are seeing to determine what is "real." It is through the wonderful and magical world of art that we come to recognize and appreciate more about the world around us.

ANSWERS

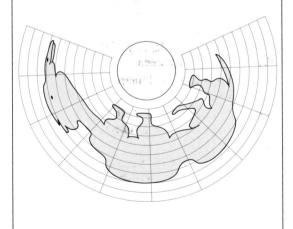

ACKNOWLEDGMENTS

PAGE 5: Salvador Dali, Spanish, 1904–1989, Mae West, gouache over photographic print, c.1934, 28.3 × 17.8cm, Gift of Mrs. Gilbert W. Chapman in memory of Charles B. Goodspeed, 1949.517 © DEMART PRO ARTE BV/DACS 1993 Photograph © 1992, The Art Institute of Chicago. All Rights Reserved.

PAGE 6: Hans Holbein the Younger, The Ambassadors, 1533, reproduced by courtesy of the Trustees, The National Gallery, London

PAGE 9: Paul Gauguin, French, 1848–1903, Old Women at Arles, oil on canvas, 1888, 73 × 92cm, Mr. and Mrs. Lewis Larned Coburn Memorial Collection, 1934.391. Photograph © 1991, The Art Institute of Chicago. All Rights Reserved.

PAGE 10–11: Anonymous, Mary, Queen of Scots Anamorphosis, National Gallery of Scotland

PAGE 13: Giuseppe Arcimboldo, Earth, by courtesy of the Bridgeman Art Library

PAGE 15: Pablo Picasso, Three Musicians, Fontainebleu, summer 1921, oil on canvas, 6'7" × 7'3¾" (200.7 × 222.9cm) Collection, The Museum of Modern Art, New York. Mrs. Simon Guggenheim Fund © DACS 1993 Photograph © 1992 The Museum of Modern Art, New York

PAGE 16: Jan van Eyck, The Arnolfini Marriage, Reproduced by courtesy of the Trustees, The National Gallery, London

PAGE 19: Parmigianino, Self-Portrait in a Convex Mirror, Kunsthistorisches Museum, Vienna

PAGES 20–21: William Scrots, Edward VI Anamorphosis, National Portrait Gallery, London

PAGE 23: Anonymous, eighteenth-century Dutch cylindrical anamorphosis of a tightrope performer, Museum Boerhaave, Leiden

PAGE 26: Anonymous, Man-of-War, cylindrical anamorphosis on wood, Reproduced by permission of the Trustees of the Science Museum, London

PAGE 27: Anonymous, Lute player, cylindrical anamorphosis, Sotheby's Book Department, London

PAGE 29: Gert Dittmers, King Frederick III and his Queen, Nationalmuseet, Copenhagen

PAGE 31: Anonymous, Charles I of England, Swedish Portrait Archives, Gripsholm. Photograph: Statens Konstmuseer

PAGE 32: Puss in Boots cylindrical anamorphosis, Sotheby's Book Department, London

PAGE 36: Salvador Dali, Paranoiac Figure, 1934–5, Private Collection © DEMART PRO ARTE BV/DACS 1993

PAGE 37: Salvador Dali, The Paranoiac Visage, from "Le Surrealism au service de la Revolution" Photo: MNAM, Centre Georges Pompidou © DEMART PRO ARTE BV/DACS 1993

PAGE 39: Sky and Water I (1938) © 1992 M.C. Escher/Cordon Art – Baarn – Holland

PAGE 41: Josse de Momper, Anamorphic Landscape, Private Collection

PAGE 43: René Magritte, Belgian, 1898–1967, Le soir qui tombe, 1964, Houston, Menil Foundation © ADGAP, Paris and DACS, London 1993 Photograph © Giraudon

PAGES 44–45: Detail, Leonardo da Vinci's notebooks, Windsor Castle, Royal Library © 1992 Her Majesty the Queen

PAGES 48, 49, 51, 52, 53, 56: Illustrations by Technical Art Services

FRONT JACKET: Johann Konig, Portrait of a Standing Man, 1628, Art Collection of the University of Uppsala

ENDPAPERS: Symmetry Drawing E 66 (1945) © 1992 M.C. Escher/Cordon Art – Baarn – Holland